This book
belongs to

....

For Manda

FREDERICK WARNE

Published by the Penguin Group
Penguin Books Ltd, 80 Strand, London WC2R 0RL, England
Penguin Young Readers Group, 345 Hudson Street,
New York, New York 10014, U.S.A.
Penguin Books Australia Ltd, 250 Camberwell Road, Camberwell,
Victoria 3124, Australia
Canada, India, New Zealand, South Africa

1 3 5 7 9 10 8 6 4 2

ISBN-13: 978 072325 848 3

Printed in Great Britain

Almond Blossom's Mystery

by Kay Woodward

Welcome to the Flower Fairy Garden!

Where are the fairies?
Where can we find them?
We've seen the fairy-rings
They leave behind them!

Is it a secret
No one is telling?
Why, in your garden
Surely they're dwelling!

No need for journeying,
Seeking afar:
Where there are flowers,
There fairies are!

Contents

Chapter One
The Longest Winter

None of the Flower Fairies could remember winter ever being *this* long. The bitterly cold weather seemed to have gone on for an eternity. It was months since they'd opened their presents beneath the decorated boughs of the Christmas tree, while the rusty colors of autumn were just a distant memory. It wouldn't have been so bad if the sun was shining, but that was missing too, hidden behind a thick layer of dull cloud.

At first the Flower Fairies, who are usually very optimistic creatures, were hopeful that spring was just around the corner. But when the cold, dreary weather continued, they became puzzled. Finally they began to worry. Would it be winter forever? Without the sun, how would their garden flourish? Would the buds and blossoms never appear? The fairies whispered in hushed voices to each other, desperate to learn the answer to the most important question of all: *Where was spring?*

There was one Flower Fairy in particular who was very concerned about the long winter, and that was Almond Blossom. Day after day, she peered up at the grim, gray sky and then looked closely at the bare branches of her tree.

"Nothing," she sighed. "Not even a bud." The pretty little fairy, no bigger than a human hand, slumped despondently against the tree trunk.

Spring was the most important event on Almond Blossom's calendar. Every year, as soon as winter

waved farewell,
the milder weather
encouraged her
delicate pink
blossoms to unfurl.
For all the other Flower
Fairies, this was the very first
sign of spring. For Almond Blossom,
it was her signal to perform the traditional
dance that heralded the new season. She so
enjoyed skipping and pirouetting around
the garden, brandishing one of her own
blossom-laden stems, to the sound of the
delighted cheers of the other fairies. It just
wouldn't be the same carrying a bare, brown
twig.

"Cheer up!" called Sycamore from his
lofty perch on a nearby tree. "Whatever
you're thinking about might never happen!"

"That's what I'm worried about," Almond

Blossom replied.
"What if spring
never happens—
ever? What then?"
Her pretty face
crumpled and
she sobbed
great,
fat tears
of sorrow.

"What'll I do? I may as well just pack up my things and leave the Flower Fairies Garden!"

Sycamore looked utterly horrified at the effect his seemingly harmless greeting had had on poor Almond Blossom, and he leaped the short distance between their trees, his gauzy wings glowing gold and green in the pale light. "There, there," he said, patting her shoulder awkwardly. Sycamore was at his happiest when fluttering and twirling

through the air, a little like the winged seeds
that whirled from his tree every autumn—
he didn't have much experience in making
glum fairies laugh. But he did
his best.

"Spring *will* come," he said
gently. "Just you wait and
see."

"That's very kind of
you, Sycamore," said
Almond Blossom,
wiping away her

tears. She grabbed a dark green leaf and blew
her nose into it noisily. "I don't know what's
got into me. I think I might be missing the
sun!" She laughed weakly.

Sycamore gave her an encouraging grin.
"Soon it'll be so sunny that you'll wish for a
cloud to come by to give you some shade!"
he said.

But the dull, cloudy, cold weather
continued. The only variation from the
grayness was the occasional sharp shower
that soaked and chilled any Flower Fairy
unlucky enough to be out in the open.

Almond Blossom tried to keep her

spirits up by practicing the steps of her spring dance, but her heart wasn't in it. Bleakly, she noticed that her fairy outfit was beginning to look very shabby. The pale pink petals of her tutu looked crumpled rather than frothy, while the ones adorning her chestnut locks were damp and bedraggled because of the rain. As for her dusky pink tunic, it had most definitely seen better days. Tansy— who was a whiz with needle and thread— offered to repair her clothes with some of

Snowdrop's snowy white petals, but Almond
Blossom politely refused. It wouldn't feel
right wearing someone else's petals. No, she
would make herself a brand-new outfit when
her own blossoms bloomed. Just as she did
every year.

Then the crisis deepened. One murky
morning, when the weather was so dark and
gloomy that the Flower Fairies had to use
pinches of precious fairy dust to light their
way, word spread around the garden that an
emergency meeting was to take place at the
blackthorn bush.

As soon as she heard the news, Almond

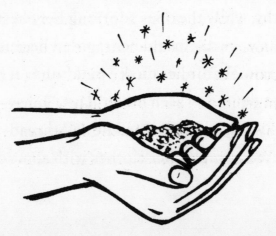

Blossom hopped down to the ground, smoothed her ragged clothes, and—peeping in a puddle on the way to make sure that she didn't look too scruffy—scurried toward the blackthorn bush. By the time she arrived, a large crowd of Flower Fairies had gathered. They muttered to each other in low voices.

"What's going on?" Almond Blossom asked Windflower, an elegant fairy with

long, dark hair and mahogany-patterned wings.

Windflower shrugged. "I heard there was going to be some big announcement," she said. "But I haven't a clue what it's about."

"Shhhh!" whispered Blackthorn. She sat on a low branch, almost hidden by the tiny white flowers that smothered her plant—one of the very few to bear flowers in this chilly weather. "Someone's coming!"

"Greetings!" A powerful voice rang out,

silencing the waiting crowd immediately. Heads swiveled round to see who had spoken, and then there was a collective gasp. A dazzling Flower Fairy stood before them. He was clothed in shimmering gold and wore a crown of yellow flower stamens on his golden hair. It was Kingcup—the king of the Flower Fairies! "Please be seated," the royal visitor continued.

Obediently, everyone sat.

Almond Blossom's throat was as dry as sandpaper, and she swallowed with difficulty. It didn't

take a fairy diploma to know that bad news
was coming.

"Flower Fairies . . . we have a problem,"
said Kingcup, his kind eyes clouded with
concern. "I'm sure you've noticed that winter
has gone on for a very long time. For some
weeks, I was convinced that it was just an
odd weather pattern and that any day we'd
see dear Almond Blossom dancing merrily
through the garden, followed swiftly by

glorious spring weather." He paused to smile briefly at her. "But now I know different. Prepare yourselves, Flower Fairies, for the truth is shocking."

Everyone held their breath.

"Spring isn't late," said Kingcup. *"Spring has been stolen!"*

Chapter Two

A Grand Plan

There was a stunned silence as the fairies absorbed the awful news. This wasn't the sort of thing that happened in the Flower Fairies Garden.

"I'm afraid there's more," said Kingcup apologetically. "Unfortunately, this year's Spring Party will have to be postponed ... until spring is restored to its rightful place. I'm most terribly sorry."

There was a strangled sob in the middle of the crowd as one Flower Fairy was overwhelmed by the bad tidings.

Shakily, Almond Blossom raised an arm into the air. "If you please, sir ..." she began.

Kingcup looked in her direction and nodded.

"It's just that ... er ... what I-I-I'd like to know ... that is, what I'm sure *everyone* w-would like to know is ..." Almond Blossom paused, wishing that she felt braver. "How do you know? Why was spring stolen? Who did it? When? And where—"

"Whoa there," said Kingcup, his handsome face creasing into a brief smile. "Let me try

to answer those
questions before
you think of
any more." He
reached into a
pocket and pulled
out a scroll of
parchment tied with a
long ribbon of grass.
Slowly, thoughtfully,
he held the
parchment aloft.
"This," he said,
"is a ransom
note. It explains
everything—I
think it's best if
I read it aloud."

There were nods of approval from
the crowd.

Dear Flower Fairies

My, what a long, cold winter! And do you know why? It's because we've stolen spring and hidden it from you. Ha ha! You'll never find it. But we're prepared to do a deal. In exchange for spring, we want six sacks filled to the brim with fairy dust.

On Saturday evening at sunset, you must leave these sacks beneath the almond tree. By Sunday morning, spring will return. No fairy dust means no spring.

Do not try to find us, or we will steal summer too.

Signed,
As if we'd tell you!

Kingcup rolled up the parchment and tucked it back into his pocket. "So, dear Flower Fairies," he said, "we have these dastardly thieves to thank for our worst ever winter. And now we need to work out what to do."

"Why that's simple!" piped up Rose, a friendly little fairy who loved to make others happy. "If everyone works extra hard, we should just about have enough fairy dust by Saturday. I have some large leaves that we could make into sturdy sacks. And perhaps the blackbirds would help by carrying the sacks from flower to flower until they are full."

"No way!" Sycamore cried indignantly. He leaped to his feet and looked stern. "We can't give in to their demands! We must send out a search party immediately and hunt high and low until we've tracked down the thieves."

"But then they'll steal summer!" wailed Daisy.

"I-I-I'm not sure we can make s-six sacks of f-fairy dust by S-S-Saturday." White Clover's round, rosy cheeks were awash with tears.

"We want to go to the Spring Party!" sobbed the Sweet Pea babies.

It was pandemonium. Everywhere Almond Blossom looked, there were Flower Fairies shouting or crying into their petal handkerchiefs. She looked around for Kingcup and saw that he was refereeing a squabble between Yew fairy and Pine Tree fairy. She scratched her head thoughtfully. If they were going to rescue spring *and* save the party, somebody needed to do something right now.

"Please be quiet!" bellowed Almond Blossom at the top of her voice. And

everyone was so astonished by the
mild-mannered fairy's command that they
stopped shouting and arguing and crying
immediately. "Thank you," she continued
meekly. "I have a plan, if anyone would
like to hear it?"

At once, a sea of heads nodded.

"Gather round," whispered Almond Blossom. "We don't want to be overheard."

By noon, it was settled. Most of the Flower Fairies would set to work making heaps of sparkling fairy dust. They decided it would be best if they obeyed the ransom letter's demands—or at least pretended to. Any enemy spies that might be lurking would be fooled into thinking that the fairies had given in, while meanwhile . . . Almond Blossom would search for spring!

"Aren't you even a tiny bit nervous?"

asked Windflower,
watching as Almond
Blossom packed a small bag
with fairy cheese, hazelnuts, and a
nutcase filled with Elderberry's sweet
juice.

Almond Blossom checked all around
before nodding. "Oh *yes*!" she said. "But I'm
excited too." It was true. She'd never done
anything like this before—never been on a
secret mission, never been trusted with such
an important task. She could hardly wait!

"What will you do?" asked Windflower.
"Where will you go?" Of all the Flower
Fairies, she was perhaps the most eager
for Almond Blossom to succeed, for her
starlike, white flowers would appear when
the first breeze of spring blew.

"First, I'm going to search the Flower
Fairies Garden thoroughly," replied Almond

Blossom, "just to make sure the thieves left no clues. Then I'll travel farther afield—and I won't stop until I've found spring." She smiled at Windflower as she shouldered her bag. "Don't worry—the blackbirds are going to fly above me. If I need help, I'll whistle for them."

"Take this," Windflower said hastily, thrusting a small, silky-soft bag

into her friend's hand. "It's fairy dust. It's not much, I'm afraid, but it's all I have. Go on, run—and take care!" She leaped from the bare branch and somersaulted through the air, landing neatly on the ground below. "Farewell!" she cried, before hurrying away.

Almond Blossom smiled as she looked at Windflower's gift. Everybody was being so kind—she just hoped that she could repay them by returning with spring.

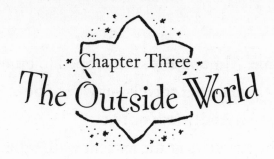

By the time Almond Blossom had finished
exploring the Flower Fairies Garden, not
a leaf or a stone or a fallen petal was left
unturned. But she didn't find a single clue.
Whoever had stolen spring had done a *very*
good job of covering their tracks.

It's time to go over the wall, thought Almond
Blossom, trudging toward the far side of
the garden. Here, the wall backed onto open
marshes, where only the occasional winding
lane interrupted the wild countryside.
Flower Fairies lived here too—among the
reeds and wild grasses and nestling under
flowers of the hedgerow and wayside. Many
of these fairies visited the garden from time

to time. Almond Blossom hoped to bump
into them on her travels—it would be lovely
to see a friendly face or two.

She gazed up at the ancient wall, relieved
to see that there were plenty of hollows to
slip her fingers and toes inside. Briskly, she
climbed up the rough stones, stopping
only when she reached the top.

"Phew!" said Almond
Blossom, perching on the
wall to admire the view.
Far below her dangling
feet was a wide, muddy
track, its surface
furrowed and
uneven. Through
the light mist
that hung
before
her, she

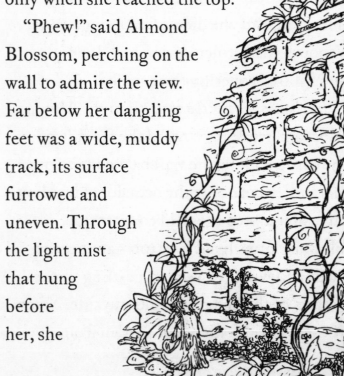

could make out a dark green hedgerow opposite. It was interwoven with bindweed—white, cushiony blooms that were bold enough and pushy enough to grow absolutely anywhere. She was wondering if White Bindweed fairy was at home when a wisp of white mist engulfed her. Brrrr! She shivered at its cold touch. It seemed as if the rest of Flower Fairyland was in winter's steely grip too. Almond Blossom couldn't help feeling a little disappointed—she'd hoped that there might be a smidgen of warmth on the other side of the wall.

Ding ding! Ding-a-ling! Ding!
Abruptly, the silence of the quiet

countryside was
shattered by a
frantic jangling of
bells.

"Hurry up, Mark!"
The anxious voice echoed along the track,
accompanied by more *ding-a-ling*-ing.
"We'll be late!"

"I'm coming!" replied another voice.

Humans! She'd never seen or heard one
before, but others had told her how big and
noisy they were. And according to Flower
Fairy law, she *must* stay out of sight. If
humans knew that fairies really did exist,
the fairies' fragile world might be crushed
underfoot by stampeding feet or harmed by
curious fingers.

With nowhere to hide and no time to flee,
Almond Blossom had no choice but to fold
her wings shut and curl herself into the

tightest possible ball. And then she waited.

The ground began to tremble horribly and there was an ear-splitting screech. "I *really* need new brakes," muttered a voice. The Flower Fairy couldn't resist peeking and saw a girl with dark, silky hair and big blue eyes. She was crouching over a bright blue contraption that Almond Blossom knew must be a bicycle. The girl's face broke into a wide grin as a younger boy skidded to a halt

beside her. They looked so much alike that they had to be sister and brother. "Where's Toby?" she asked.

"Not far away," replied the boy. "He was barking at some mushrooms a little way back. Oh, here he comes!"

A caramel-colored dog with floppy ears bounded out of the mist, sitting—*splat!*—in a puddle beside the children. He panted, his tongue lolling to one side.

I don't know what all the fuss is about, Almond Blossom thought to herself. *Humans seem perfectly harmless. Pleasant, even. And I rather like their d—*

Woof! Woof-woof!
Toby the dog had
begun to make
the most awful
racket that
she'd ever

heard. *Ow-ow-ow-WOOOOO!* he howled.

Almond Blossom's heart sank as, too late, she remembered how finely tuned animals' senses were. Now the dog was staring right at Almond Blossom. He'd seen her!

"What is it, Toby?" asked the boy. "You silly dog! There aren't any mushrooms up there... or *are* there?" He stood on tiptoe and squinted at the top of the wall.

Any second now, they would start clambering toward her, and then they would find her, and before nightfall she would be on display in a museum—Almond Blossom just knew it! Unless... Quickly, she delved her hand deep into the silken bag that

Windflower had given her. She scooped a handful of the precious fairy dust into her palm and blew with all her might.

Whoosh!

A cloud of tiny pollen fragments billowed outward.

"Fairy dust, fairy dust, hide me from sight!" Almond Blossom whispered. At once, the air all around her began to glimmer and shimmer magically.

"What are you looking at, Mark?" asked the girl curiously.

"Er . . . nothing," replied her brother.

"I could have sworn that I saw something . . ."
He paused and frowned, scratching his head.
"Something really strange. But now it's gone.
I must have been mistaken."

Toby the dog had stopped barking now

and was happily snuffling at the children's feet.

Almond Blossom smiled to herself. "Thank you, Windflower," she whispered in the tiniest of voices. The fairy dust had worked its magic brilliantly—she was *totally* shielded from view.

"Come on, then," said the girl. "Let's escape this murky weather—I want to see the sun again." She leaped back onto her bicycle. "Race you?"

As the children and their dog vanished around the corner, Almond Blossom rubbed her chin thoughtfully. Something was bothering her, but she couldn't for the life of her work out what it was.

Chapter Four
A Big Adventure

Almond Blossom peered into the darkening gloom. This was not good. Night was falling and she hadn't even reached the marsh yet. And with only two days to go before Saturday's deadline, she didn't have a moment to lose. She grasped a piece of ivy that clung to the stone wall and expertly slid down its length, landing with a tiny *splish* on the sodden ground below.

Shouldering her bag once more, she skipped and fluttered across the track to the safety of the hedgerow.

"Yoohoo!" shouted White Bindweed, who was busy weaving flowers in and out of the hedge. "Are you staying for tea?"

"That's very kind of you," replied Almond Blossom, "but I can't stop. I'm searching for spring."

"Oh, I see . . ." said White Bindweed, screwing up her face as if she didn't really see at all. She shrugged and grinned. "Okay, then. Catch you later!"

Almond Blossom fought her way through the hedge, which for someone as small as a Flower Fairy was more like a huge and very spooky forbidden forest. Sturdy branches blocked her path, while twigs sprang at her and tore her already tattered clothes. And it was *so* dark. Bravely she pushed on, reminding herself that the happiness of the Flower Fairies *and* the magnificent Spring Party were at stake. She *had* to succeed.

At last, she reached the other side of the hedge. The overcast sky was charcoal gray now—soon it would be black—but there was just enough light for Almond Blossom to see a little way. She plunked herself down on a handy rock and admired the view. So this was the fabled marsh. A carpet of moss stretched away from her, dotted with clumps of tall grass. Large, lumpy shapes loomed in the distance. For a moment, she feared they might be giants or ogres or some other scary creatures, but then she realized that they were probably just trees. She giggled to herself, as excitement fizzed through her once more.

This was a grand adventure, all right.

"Time to go!" she announced to the empty wilderness. She leaped to her feet and marched away from the hedge, trying hard not to lose her balance on the springy moss.

Almond Blossom soon learned that while the Flower Fairies Garden was quite flat, the marsh was a totally different story. Hollows nestled between grassy hillocks, some of which were mountainous. She struggled to the top of the highest of these mounds, deciding that it would be a perfect spot to camp for the night. But when she reached the top, all thoughts of sleep instantly vanished from her mind.

"What *is* it?" breathed the little Flower Fairy. A bright stripe of sparkling color split the darkness, stretching from left to right across the distant horizon. Almond Blossom had never seen anything so wonderful. It glittered like the brightest jewel and burned as bright as the biggest candle. It was vivid pink and luscious orange and deepest mauve.

It was beautiful.

But she still didn't know what it *was*. Dazzled and bewildered, Almond Blossom sank onto the comfortable moss and stared. Little by little, the mysterious glow faded from view, the colors darkening, the light dimming . . . until it was gone. Then, tired beyond belief, she slept.

"Wakey, wakey, rise and shine!" sang a friendly voice.

"Hmmm?" groaned Almond Blossom. She looked up groggily to see two of the scruffiest Flower Fairies she'd ever laid eyes on staring down at her. "Who are you?" she asked.

"I'm Rush-Grass," announced the dark-haired fairy. He reached down to shake Almond Blossom's hand, pumping it up and down enthusiastically. "Pleased to meet you."

"And I'm Cotton-Grass," said the other fairy, with a cheeky grin. His hair was ash

blond and stood up from his head as if he'd had a very big fright. "We're brothers."

Almond Blossom smiled back, noticing absentmindedly that the two Flower Fairies

had *very* pointy ears. And although their wings were quite plain, their clothes blended in perfectly with the colors of the marsh grasses—chestnut brown, moss green, and deep maroon. In fact, they seemed so much at home on the marsh that she knew without asking that they must be locals.

"You're not from around here, are you?"

said Rush-Grass, reminding her that she hadn't introduced herself yet.

"Oh, I'm sorry," she said. "How very rude of me. I'm Almond Blossom—I come from the Flower Fairies Garden." She sprang to her feet and curtsied politely.

"There's no need for that," said Cotton-Grass, with a stifled giggle. "You're on the marsh now—we're much more laid back here than the fairies in your garden." He gave his brother a sideways glance. "Are *you* going to ask her?"

Rush-Grass nodded. "What are you *doing* here?" he asked curiously. "Are you lost? Because if you're lost, we'd be delighted to lead you to safety. That's our job, you see."

Almond Blossom shook her head.

"And if you're *not* lost," added Cotton-Grass, "then we're pretty good guides too. We can show you all the sights—the twisty marsh path, the fairy rings, the elves' secret hideaway, Mallow's famous fairy cheese—"

"What?" Almond Blossom spluttered. Of course! How could she have been so forgetful?

"It's delicious," said Cotton-Grass, rubbing his tummy and making *mmmmm* noises. "Mallow's seeds make the most excellent cheese—the best in Flower Fairyland—"

"No, not the *cheese*," interrupted Almond Blossom again. "The elves!

Can you help me to find them?"

"But of course," replied Rush-Grass. He gave an exasperated sigh and rolled his eyes. "What have they done now?" he asked.

"Well, they may have done *nothing*," began Almond Blossom uncertainly. She was a very fair fairy and liked to give everyone a chance, but the elves were well known throughout the Flower Fairies Garden for their tricks and monkey business. Stealing spring would be just the sort of mischief they loved. "I have a feeling that they might be able to point me in the right direction," she added. Noticing that the brothers were looking quite confused, Almond Blossom told them how the Flower Fairies had received a ransom note and there were no clues in their garden, so she'd ventured over the wall and onto the marsh to search for any sign of spring or the wicked thieves who'd stolen it. "Surely you must have noticed how long winter has lasted?" she said.

"Oh, yes," said Cotton-Grass. "The weather's dreadful here, isn't it?" He looked up at the thick gray clouds above them. "It's much nicer on the other side of the marsh. We should take you there." He pointed. "Look!"

Almond Blossom looked. She blinked. Then she looked again. There, in the distance, was a sunny strip of yellow, just visible at the edge of the low, gray cloud. Was it...? Could it really be...? It was!

"Hurray!" she cheered, fluttering into the air with joy. "It's springtime! We've found *spring*!"

Chapter Five

Caught!

At once, everything slotted into place . . .
Spring hadn't been stolen—it was simply
hidden behind a thick blanket of gray cloud.
This explained why the children had hurried
to escape the murky weather and find the
sun. It also explained why it seemed as if
winter had lasted so long this year.

"The beautiful stripe of color was the
sunset," breathed Almond Blossom. It
was such an age since she'd
seen the evening sun, she'd
forgotten how magnificent it
could be. She was so pleased
that she couldn't resist a
happy skip and a hop,
much to the delight of

her new fairy friends.

Then she sat down and thought. And
thought. But no matter how she puzzled and
pondered, mused and mulled it over,
she kept coming back to the same conclusion.
Whoever had sent the ransom note to the
Flower Fairies must *also* have hung the great
dark cloud above their garden.

"Will you help me to find the thieves?"
she asked the marsh fairies. "I want to ask
the elves what they know, but I don't know
where to find them."

Rush-Grass and Cotton-Grass nodded
solemnly.

"We'll take you there as soon as you've had breakfast," said Rush-Grass sensibly. "It's really not a good idea to do this sort of thing on an empty stomach."

So as soon as Almond Blossom had nibbled a hazelnut and sipped the cool spring

water that Cotton-Grass had brought her, they set off across the marsh. They trekked past tall waving grasses and around squidgy bogs, the two brothers making sure that she

didn't stray away from the path and into danger.

It didn't take long to reach the edge of the cloud, where the marsh was bathed in glorious sunshine. Almond Blossom paused for a moment, closing her eyes and raising her face up to the gentle warmth of the sun.

"There," Cotton-Grass whispered.

Almond Blossom blinked a little as her eyes got used to the brightness. "Where?" she whispered back, scanning the area all around them.

Cotton-Grass pointed to an innocent-looking cluster of toadstools a short distance away.

They were quite the prettiest things Almond Blossom had seen all morning, with their chocolatey-brown stems and their cherry-red caps, dotted all over with large white spots. The colors dazzled in the spring sunshine.

"Quite poisonous, of course," muttered Rush-Grass. "And the perfect place for those naughty elves to hide their secret headquarters."

"We don't *know* that they've done anything wrong," said Almond Blossom.

"Hmmm." Cotton-Grass didn't sound so sure. "Then let's go and find out," he said, marching toward the toadstools. But before they even reached the elves' secret hideaway, gleeful voices rang out loud and clear.

"We've *fooled* them!"

"Tomorrow we'll have *six sacks* of fairy dust!"

"We are *so* clever! Ha ha *haaa*!"

Almond Blossom crept closer and peered between the toadstools. And there, in a small clearing, were three green-clad creatures with pointy ears and pointy wings. They were laughing fit to burst. "You're not that clever," she said sweetly.

The elves spun around. "Oh," said the tallest of the three.

"Oh, indeed," said Almond Blossom, squeezing through a narrow gap into the hideaway. She put her hands on her hips and frowned at the guilty-looking trio. "Why did you do it?" she asked.

"We only wanted some fairy dust,"

mumbled the shortest elf, staring down at his feet. "It's not fair, you know," he said.

"You Flower Fairies have all the fun, with your singing and dancing in your *wonderful* garden."

He looked up and glared at Almond Blossom, who was suddenly feeling a little sorry for the miserable creatures.

"We thought it would be funny if we were enjoying the lovely spring weather, while you were stuck under a wintry cloud," he continued. "And it *was* funny. We haven't been able to *stop* laughing." He looked at his two sidekicks. "Have we, lads?"

"Er, yes . . ." said the tall elf quickly. "I mean, no, boss."

"Ho ho ho," the third elf laughed unconvincingly. "Hee hee."

"But why did you write the ransom note?" asked Almond Blossom, curious now. "Why didn't you just hide the sun and be done with it? Why did you want the fairy dust too? Elves have their own magic

dust, don't they?"

"It's not as sparkly as yours," grumbled the chief elf. "And it's not quite as magical either. Besides, we've only got about a thimbleful left—it took heaps of elf dust to cast the Winter Cloud Spell." He paused and looked suddenly cunning. "Why don't you tell us how to make fairy dust? Because if we knew how to make it, we wouldn't need yours, would we?"

"Nice try!" Almond Blossom laughed. "But I'm afraid that only Flower Fairies can make fairy dust—and how we make it is a closely guarded secret."

"Hmmmph," said the elf.

Almond Blossom thought deeply. Here was a problem indeed. How was she to convince the elves to lift the cloud that covered the Flower Fairies Garden *without* collecting the six sacks of fairy dust they'd demanded? Unless . . .

Almond Blossom pulled out the silky bag that Windflower had given her. "Listen very carefully," she said mysteriously. "I have an idea."

Chapter Six
Back to the Garden

Almond Blossom ran her fingertips over her velvet-soft tunic and gently touched the tiny petals sewn around the neck. Then she whirled around, grinning with delight as the pink petals of her skirt spun outward. Her new outfit was perfect.

She was ready.

Carefully breaking off a twig from her tree—she made sure to choose one that was heavily laden with brand-new blossoms—

Almond Blossom
clutched it tightly
before leaping into the air.
Gracefully, she fluttered
downward, landing lightly far
below, where green shoots were
beginning to poke through the soil.
Almond Blossom raised herself on
tiptoes, took a deep breath, and began to
sing the words that the Flower Fairies had
waited so long to hear:

"*Joy! The Winter's nearly gone!*
Soon will Spring come dancing on;
And before her, here dance I,
Pink like sunrise in the sky.
Other lovely things will follow;
Soon will cuckoo come, and swallow;
Birds will sing and buds will burst,
But the Almond is the first!"

Happily, she danced through the garden, twirling and high-stepping as she went, hopping and leaping, spinning and swaying.

"Almond Blossom!" cried Sycamore as she jigged past. "Am I glad to see you! Does this mean that spring is officially on the way?"

In reply, she pointed to the east, where the early morning sun was rising above the horizon, turning the wispy clouds above them the same shade of pink as her pretty blossoms.

"Hurray!" cheered Sycamore, bouncing up and down on a branch. Then he stopped. "But what happened to the nasty winter weather? Did we

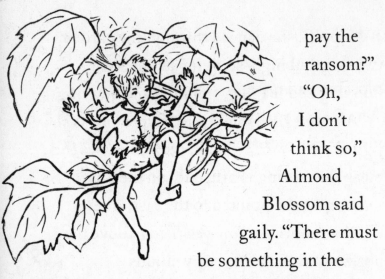

pay the
ransom?"
"Oh,
I don't
think so,"
Almond
Blossom said
gaily. "There must
be something in the
air, I suppose." She waved her flowery twig.
"Must dash! Don't forget about the Spring
Party!" She chuckled gleefully as she danced
away, leaving a stunned Sycamore behind
her.

Everything had turned out so well.
Understandably, the elves had been dubious
about her idea at first. They were utterly
dazzled by the expectation of the six
wonderful sacks of magical fairy dust that
awaited them, and they were unwilling to

give them up.
But Almond
Blossom had made
them feel so guilty
with stories of the
heartbroken Flower
Fairies with tears
dripping down their
cheeks as they pined
for spring that they
gave in at last and agreed

to lift the Winter Cloud Spell. Because
their stocks of elf dust were so low, Almond
Blossom had handed over the little silken
bag—there were still a couple of handfuls of
Windflower's precious fairy dust left —and
made the elves promise to use it wisely,
before she hitched a lift home with a friendly
blackbird.

Now, as she admired the glorious morning

sky, Almond Blossom saw that the elves had kept their word.

"*Joy! The winter's nearly gone!*" she sang again, continuing her merry dance.

The Flower Fairies were so eager for the new season to arrive that the Spring Party was held only a few days later. The garden was decked with as many flowers as Almond Blossom could spare and bunches of sunny yellow daffodils. Wildflower's tiny white flowers were scattered over the ground like fallen stars, while swathes of newly opened bluebells stretched as far as the eye could see. So much extra fairy dust had been made that week, it was sprinkled here and there. The glade gleamed and twinkled everywhere the Flower Fairies looked.

It was a wonderful party. Lots of familiar faces joined in the fun, but there were some

unfamiliar faces too. Rush-Grass and
Cotton-Grass had made the long journey

across the marsh—they turned out to be
excellent dancers—and three more visitors
weren't far behind.

The elves smiled sheepishly at Almond
Blossom as they sipped Elderberry's famous
juice from buttercups. "Thank you for
inviting us," mumbled the chief elf, fiddling
with his cuff.

"We love to dance," said the second elf, who was unable to stop his feet from tapping.

"We just never get the chance," said the third elf. "Thank you."

"It's the least I could do," Almond Blossom replied. "After all, you did return spring to us!"

And with that she winked at the elves and fluttered across to join her fairy friends at her favorite party of the year.

FLOWER FAIRIES FRIENDS™

Visit our Flower Fairies website at:

www.flowerfairies.com

There are lots of fun Flower Fairy games and activities for you to play, plus you can find out more about all your favorite fairy friends!

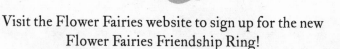

Log onto the
Flower Fairies
Friendship Ring

Visit the Flower Fairies website to sign up for the new Flower Fairies Friendship Ring!

★ No membership fee
★ News and updates
★ Every new friend receives a special gift!
(while supplies last)

More tales from these Flower Fairies coming soon!

Candytuft

Strawberry

Jasmine

Sweet Pea